D
M
c
R
r
d
C
e
I0816727
m
k
H
h
K
E

Hen
Cat
Hen and Cat

Cat and Hen pack a picnic.

Snacks, dip, cress, and ten mints in a tin

□ a pack
□ a stick
□ a red hat

Hen and Cat skip...

...and trek...

...and pant...

...and sit.

Hen picks a snack.
Mmmm, crisp!

Cat sits and drips.

a sad, damp cat